Two Can Share, Too

By Janelle Cherrington
Based on a Teleplay by Andy Yerkes
Illustrated by Normand Chartier

Simon Spotlight

Based on the TV series *Bear in the Big Blue House*™
created by Mitchell Kriegman. Produced by
The Jim Henson Company for Disney Channel.

SIMON SPOTLIGHT
An imprint of Simon & Schuster Children's Publishing Division
1230 Avenue of the Americas
New York, New York 10020

Manufactured in the United States of America
First Edition   10 9 8 7 6
ISBN 0-689-82330-4

Things were quiet at the Big Blue House.

Pip and Pop were swimming in the otter pond.

Tutter was in the kitchen making his famous seven-decker peanut butter and jelly sandwich.

Ojo and Treelo were playing together in the living room, and Bear was arranging a big bunch of freshly cut daisies. Bears love the smell of fresh flowers!

"Isn't it great to have friends who play together and get along so well?" Bear thought to himself.

Then, all of a sudden . . .

"BEAAAAAAR!" yelled Ojo and Treelo.

Bear turned to see what was wrong.

"Yes, Ojo? Yes, Treelo? Can I be of help?" asked Bear.

"Well, Bear," Ojo began. "Treelo *was* playing with his feather, but then he decided he wanted to play with Snow Bear instead. But Snow Bear's mine! She's mine, mine, mine, and I don't want Treelo to play with her!"

"Okay, Ojo," Bear said. "Now let me hear what Treelo has to say."
"I want Snow Bear! I want Snow Bear!" said Treelo.

"Hmm. Maybe you could trade for a little while," Bear said. "Treelo could play with Snow Bear, and Ojo could play with Treelo's feather," Bear added as they followed him through the hallway and into the kitchen.

"NO, BEAR!" yelled Ojo. "I don't want to trade! Treelo doesn't even know the kinds of things Snow Bear likes to do!"

"Okay, okay. Just let me think about this for a minute while I get these flowers some water."

Sure enough, by the time the vase was full, Bear had a plan.

"I suppose it would be hard to think of a way that *both* of you can play with Snow Bear at the same time," he began. "You're right, Ojo," he continued, nodding his big bear head. "It would be silly for you and Treelo to even *think* about playing 'Snow Bear in the Woods.'"

"Snow Bear in Woods?" said Treelo.

"What's 'Snow Bear in the Woods'?" Ojo asked.

"It's a great game I used to play with my own snow bear when I was little," Bear said.

"Really?" asked Ojo. "How do you play?"

"Well," Bear began, "first we pretend that Snow Bear is walking through the woods with her friend, umm, let's see . . . her good friend Ojo."

"Ojo? That's me, Bear!" Ojo said.

"That's right, Ojo. It is you," Bear said with a smile.

"So, maybe Snow Bear and her friend Ojo are walking through the woods, and they hear a strange sound, way, way up in the trees," Bear continued.

"What sound? What sound, Bear?" Treelo asked.

"They stop and look up—way, way up," Bear said. "And they see something blue and green and white. It looks like a . . . a friendly little lemur!"

"Me! Me! Me!" Treelo shouted.

"Hey, that's right, Bear! Treelo is the friendly little lemur," said Ojo.

"I know, Bear. I know what happens next," Ojo continued. "Maybe they all walk together until they all slide down a muddy hill and land right in . . . "

"Otter pond! Otter pond!" said Treelo.

"Hey, Bear, this is fun!" Ojo said. "Treelo, let's go outside to the otter pond!"

"Heh, heh, heh," Bear laughed, as he reached to close the kitchen door behind them. But before the latch could click . . .

"BEAAAAAAR!"

"Uh-oh. I hope everything is okay," Bear thought to himself as he headed toward the pond.

"Hi, Bear!" said Pip and Pop as Bear walked up.

"Glad you could make it, Bear, glad you could make it!" said Tutter. "We want you to come join the fun."

"It's a great day—" said Pip.

"For swimming," finished Pop.

"Or swinging," said Treelo.

"Or playing '*A Picnic with* Snow Bear in the Woods,'" Ojo said as Bear sat down.

"Would you like some of my seven-decker peanut butter and jelly sandwich, Bear? This mouse does make a mean sandwich," Tutter offered.

"Why, thank you, Tutter, I think I will," Bear said as he leaned back to share a wonderful afternoon with his friends.